Oh Honestly, Angela!

Oh Honestly, Angela!

NANCY K. ROBINSON

SCHOLASTIC
HARDCOVER

Scholastic Inc., New York

Library of Congress Cataloging in Publication Data

Robinson, Nancy K.
Oh Honestly, Angela!

Summary: Eleven-year-old Tina works hard to convince her family
that they should make sacrifices to help the poor and needy children of
the world.
    1. Children's stories, American. [1. Charities–Fiction. 2. Family life
–Fiction] I. Title.
PZ7.R567540h 1985   [Fic]   85-2102
                    ISBN 0-590-32983-9

12 11 10 9 8 7 6 5 4 3 2   6 7 8 9/8 0/9

                    Printed in the U.S.A.   12

To my little sister, Patty....

Contents

A Dark and Stormy Day

On a Monday morning two weeks before Christmas, Angela was awakened by the crash of thunder. She looked out her window. It was morning, but there were dark clouds in the sky and a strange yellowish light. Suddenly she saw a flash of lightning. Large drops of rain splattered against her window. A few seconds later the rain came down in sheets. The room became almost as dark as night.

Angela did not think it was supposed to thunder and lightning in the middle of winter. She wondered if her kindergarten would be called off today.

Angela hugged her stuffed elephant and slid

down under the covers. Stuffed Elephant always made her feel safer. He was a small white elephant with a red bow and red pads on his feet. He was so precious he didn't even have a name. No name was good enough for Stuffed Elephant.

Suddenly Angela noticed a big lump in her bed. Angela held very still and watched the lump. It was moving. It was squeezing closer to her. Angela gave the lump a sharp kick.

"Ouch!" said the lump. Angela watched in amazement as her older sister Tina lifted her head from under the covers.

"Oh, Tina!" Angela cried. "How come you're in my bed? Did you have another bad dream?"

"I had a horrible dream," Tina said.

The rain beat loudly against the window. Angela shivered, but, at the same time, she felt warm and cozy. Her big sister was eleven years old and needed *her*.

Tina stretched out next to her little sister and stared up at the ceiling. "I dreamt there was no Christmas," she said.

Angela felt a chill creep up her neck, but she said calmly, "How come?"

"Well," Tina began, "in the dream it was Christmas Eve. We decorated the tree, we sang

Christmas carols, we hung up our stockings, and we left a plate of cookies for Santa . . ."

". . . and a glass of milk?" Angela asked, wanting to make sure everything in the dream had been done correctly.

"Yes," Tina said, "and a glass of milk. There I was, lying in bed, trying to go to sleep —"

"Were you counting sheep?" Angela asked. Angela often put herself to sleep by counting sheep. Tina had taught her that trick. But Angela's sheep did not jump over fences. Angela was afraid that some of them—especially the little lambs—might break their legs. So she counted sheep jumping rope. It worked out just as well.

Tina thought for a minute. "No," she said slowly, "I wasn't counting sheep—I was looking out the window when I suddenly noticed that the stars were moving. . . ."

"The stars were moving?" Angela asked.

"Yes," Tina said. "They were moving very fast across the sky."

Angela wasn't sure she wanted to hear any more. But Tina went on: "The next thing I knew it was the next morning, but it wasn't Christmas; it was just another day. Dad was shaving, Mom was in the kitchen, and you and Nathaniel were getting ready for school. 'What about Christmas?' I asked. 'What happened to Christmas?' Everyone laughed and said, 'We already *had* Christmas, Tina. Don't you remember? You must have missed it. *It must have slipped your mind.'* "

"Oh," Angela said. She had goosebumps all over. "That's the worst dream you ever had!"

"Do you really think so?" Tina asked modestly.

"Yes," Angela said. She was quiet for a moment. Then she said, "Um . . . Tina . . . when *is* Christmas?"

"You mean really?" Tina asked.

Angela nodded.

"Well, it's not next Monday; it's the Monday after. Christmas is in two weeks," Tina told her.

Angela breathed a sigh of relief. "Well, then, we didn't miss it," she said.

To her surprise, Tina laughed and hugged her.

"Will Daddy be back in time?" Angela asked. Their father was away on a concert tour. He played the cello in the city orchestra.

"Of course," Tina said. "He's coming back the day after tomorrow—Wednesday."

A crash of thunder made both girls jump. There was more lightning, and the rain beat down harder than ever. The wind howled around their apartment building.

Suddenly the doorbell rang. Tina clutched Angela. It rang again.

"Someone's at the door!" Tina whispered in terror.

For a moment Angela was frightened, too. Everything seemed so creepy this morning.

"It's only Nathaniel," Angela reassured her big sister. "I bet he forgot his keys."

Nathaniel was the oldest. He was thirteen years old and went to junior high school. He left for school much earlier than Tina and Angela.

Angela jumped out of bed and padded across the floor in her pajama feet. "I'll answer it," she told Tina.

Tina looked at the Bugs Bunny clock on Angela's bed table. They would have to start getting ready for school soon. She put her head down on Angela's pillow and tried to figure out why the words, *It must have slipped your mind,* were even scarier than the idea of missing Christmas.

Tina suddenly realized that five minutes had gone by, but Angela wasn't back.

Tina got out of Angela's bed and went into the front hall.

The hallway was dark. And, above the sound of the storm, Tina could hear heavy pounding on the front door.

"Angela!" Tina called out. "Where are you?"

She felt for the light switch, and her hand touched the molding on the door of the hall closet. Suddenly the closet door creaked open. A hand reached out and pulled Tina into the closet.

"Tina!" Angela's voice was muffled by the coats in the closet. "Don't answer the door. It's not Nathaniel!"

Tina's heart was pounding. She opened her mouth, but no words came out.

Angela went on in a horrified voice: "It's Ralph the doorman. *And he saw me in my pajamas!*"

"So you slammed the door in his face, right?" Tina asked.

"Of course I did," Angela said indignantly.

"Oh honestly, Angela!" Tina left the closet and went to the front door.

"He's going to see you in your pajamas, too!" Angela called from inside the closet.

Tina opened the front door.

"I'm sorry," she told Ralph the doorman. "You see, my sister is a little shy."

"I know it's early," Ralph said in his gloomy

voice, "but I have to get this letter to your mother right away. It's very important."

"She's still asleep," Tina said. "I'll give it to her," and she held out her hand for the letter.

"It would be better if I gave it to her in person," Ralph said. "I'm afraid I know what's in this letter. Bad news."

Tina was sure something had happened to her father.

"Who's at the door?"

Tina turned around and saw her mother standing in the hallway in her bathrobe. Her mother brushed past her and took the letter from Ralph.

"You should have gotten this weeks ago, Mrs. Steele," Ralph said. "Mrs. Steede on the third floor got it by mistake." He shook his head sadly. "Well, it looks like they finally caught up with you."

Her mother was staring at the envelope.

"From the County Courthouse?" she asked. "I don't understand." She tore open the envelope. "It's a summons!" she said. "They want me down at the courthouse. But I didn't *do* anything. . . ." She read it over. "Oh *that*!" she said.

It must be a small crime, Tina told herself. *A*

parking ticket or something like that.

Then she remembered that they didn't have a car.

"I served my time a few years ago," Ralph said sadly.

Tina stared at Ralph. Had Ralph served time in prison? Was her mother going to jail?

Her mother was still staring down at the summons. "Oh no," she said. "I'm supposed to be down there this morning!"

"Listen, Mrs. Steele," the doorman said. "Maybe if you tell them you have young children at home, they'll let you off."

"I'm afraid it's too late," her mother said. "Thanks anyway, Ralph," and she closed the door on Ralph's gloomy face.

"Tina," she said grimly. "I have to get dressed right away."

Tina's head began to clear. She suddenly felt calm. This was an emergency.

"Won't you need a lawyer?" she asked her mother in a very capable, grown-up voice.

"I'm afraid a lawyer can't help me now." Her mother sighed and looked out the window. "I don't even know how to reach your father. Well, at least he'll be back the day after tomorrow."

Tina stood in the hallway while her mother ran to get dressed. Then she went to the closet and opened the door. Angela was huddled on the floor. She stared up at Tina. Her eyes looked enormous.

"Look, Angela," Tina said. She tried to arrange her face into a peaceful, motherly smile. "There's absolutely nothing to worry about."

"You don't have to pretend," Angela said. "I already know. I know Mommy's going to jail."

"I'm sure it's a mistake," Tina said. "It doesn't make sense." But nothing made sense. It occurred to her that the children of criminals must always be surprised when they found out the truth about their parents.

"Tina," Angela said. "Do you think we're having a dream?"

"No," Tina said. "This is real."

"I thought so," Angela said. "Um . . . could you please close the door?"

"Do you want to stay in the closet?" Tina asked.

"Yes, please," Angela said. "I want to think." Tina closed the door.

A few minutes later her mother came into the hallway wearing her best dark blue suit and her silky white blouse. She was even wearing her pearls. She handed Tina a shopping list written on an envelope. Then she took two twenty-dollar bills out of her purse.

"Do you think you could do the shopping after school?" she asked Tina. "We haven't a thing in the house."

"Sure," Tina said.

"Now, make sure Angela gets up right away," her mother went on. "You know how slow she can be about getting dressed."

Tina nodded. She was all choked up.

"You look nice," she whispered to her mother.

"Thank you," her mother said. She sighed. "You know, Tina," she said, "in many ways I don't want to get out of it."

"You don't?" Tina asked.

"No, I feel I owe it—you know, to other people, to society. I feel it's my duty to serve."

Tina felt a flicker of pride. At least her mother wasn't running away. She was willing to face up to her crime.

"In fact," her mother went on, "I'm sort of excited. I've always wanted to do it. Everyone I know who's gone there says it's a very interesting experience. You meet very interesting people."

Tina was shocked. She could see how some people might think that burglars and murderers were interesting, but it didn't seem fair of her mother to actually *want* to go to jail.

Tina could not control herself anymore.

"Mom!" she burst out. "What did you do?"

"What do you mean?" her mother asked.

"What did you do wrong?"

"I didn't do anything wrong." Her mother was puzzled. "Any citizen can be called to jury duty."

"Jury duty?" Tina said vaguely. "I've heard of that. We studied it at school." She stared at her mother. "But what about jail? Aren't you going to jail?"

"Well, I will be going to jail if I don't get out of here on time," her mother said. Then she stopped and looked at Tina.

"Tina, whatever made you think I was going to jail?" she asked.

"The way Ralph talked about serving time," Tina mumbled, "and the stuff about letting you off."

"Oh Tina, how awful!" her mother said. "I thought you knew what was going on. People always talk that way about jury duty. It's a little silly, I guess." She put her arms around Tina.

"There's nothing to worry about. It's not so different from having a job, but jury duty usually only lasts two weeks. I should be home for dinner every night."

Then she said, "You really thought I was going to jail?"

"Yes," Tina said in a shaky voice, "for Christmas."

• Suddenly her mother burst out laughing. "Oh, Tina, how could you—"

"Well, I thought so, too!" screamed a voice from the closet, "and it's not funny! *Stop laughing, Mommy!*"

The Sharing Circle

Tina helped Angela get dressed. She used the last eggs in the house to make them scrambled eggs for breakfast. Then she left a note for her older brother Nathaniel. She felt very efficient.

Meanwhile she tried to explain jury duty to her little sister. Tina had suddenly become an expert (with a little help from her social studies book, *Citizens, One and All*).

"You see, Angela, anyone accused of a crime in a free country has the right to a trial by jury," Tina said as she struggled to get Angela's rubber boots on over her shoes.

Angela held very still and listened.

"A person is innocent until proven guilty,"

Tina went on. "The jury is made up of twelve people who decide if there is enough evidence to prove that person is guilty."

"Did they pick Mommy for jury duty because she is such a good citizen?" Angela asked.

"No," Tina told her. "Any citizen can be picked. They want all kinds of people — ordinary people, every-day citizens. Do you understand?"

Angela nodded. "I guess they picked Mommy because she is such a good citizen. . . ."

Tina laughed. She was proud of her mother, too.

". . . maybe the best citizen in the whole city." Angela's eyes were shining.

Angela knew all about being a good citizen from Miss Berry's kindergarten class. Good citizens did not throw blocks. Good citizens were quiet during meetings and always raised their hands when they wanted to speak.

And, at the end of each week, good citizens got a reward. They got their own personal smelly sticker. Angela always picked strawberry. She kept them in a box and was very careful not to scratch them and sniff them too much.

"Eddie Bishop is not a good citizen," Angela told Tina. "He doesn't even care about smelly

14

stickers. All he does is run around and ruin everything for everyone else. Miss Berry can't do a thing with him."

Tina was a little tired of hearing stories about Eddie Bishop. Once, Tina had seen Eddie running around the gym with a pair of enormous floppy sneakers over his shoes. Everyone had to wear sneakers in the gym. Tina was sure Eddie's family was too poor to buy him his own pair.

She looked up at the clock. It was getting late. Her friends, Melissa and Sarah, were probably already waiting for them at the corner. And, even in nice weather, Melissa did not like to be kept waiting. Tina could just hear Melissa saying to Sarah, "Tina always makes us late . . ." and then, "You know, Sarah, Tina's been getting on my nerves lately. . . ."

"We'd better hurry," Tina said. "Melissa's going to be furious."

Angela shrugged. Melissa Glenn was not one of her favorite people. Sarah was nice to her, but Melissa treated her like a package that had to be dropped off.

"Well?" Melissa asked coldly when Tina and Angela arrived at the corner.

"I'm sorry we're late," Tina began, "but, you see, my mother—"

Melissa was staring down at Tina's brown rubber boots. "Those boots are really attractive," Melissa said sarcastically. "I thought you told me you were getting new ones."

"I am," Tina murmured, "but not until Christmas."

"It's her only Christmas present," Angela explained, "because the boots she wants are so 'spensive."

Tina blushed. She had asked for boots exactly like the ones Melissa had—tan suede boots with sheepskin linings. They cost $55.

Once again, Tina tried to tell them about her mother and jury duty, but Melissa cut her off.

"That's really interesting, Tina," she said, "we're all so happy for you. But, in case you didn't notice, it happens to be raining," and she turned around and started walking.

"Don't feel bad," Sarah whispered. "She's just in a bad mood. Her mother wants her to go to this ballet tonight, but Melissa doesn't want to go."

Tina didn't say another word to Melissa on the walk to school. And she stayed far away from her for the rest of the day.

Angela was looking forward to telling her class and Miss Berry the exciting news about her mother. When it was time for the Sharing Circle, she ran and sat down on a chair right in the middle. She raised her hand.

Then she had to wait for everyone else to sit down. She was pleased when the most grown-up girl in Miss Berry's kindergarten, Cheryl White, sat down right next to her.

Just then, Chris, who was a little clumsy, bumped into Cheryl's chair. Cheryl glared at him and said in her nasal voice, "Oh Chris, what's your problem?"

Angela loved it when Cheryl said, "What's your problem?" like that. If someone pushed into Cheryl while they were lining up, Cheryl did not scream or kick or tell the teacher. She just turned around, stared at them in a bored way, and said, very slowly, "What's your problem?"

Angela often practiced saying, "What's your problem?" the way Cheryl said it, but she never remembered to say it at the right time.

She kept her hand raised and tried to think of something grown-up to say to Cheryl.

Everyone was sitting down in the Sharing Circle now, except for Eddie. Eddie never sat down in the Sharing Circle. He preferred throwing blocks or doing anything that made a lot of noise. Today he was playing the drums with the pots and pans in the home corner. That gave Angela an idea of what to say to Cheryl.

"That Eddie Bishop!" Angela said, shaking her head sadly.

"You're telling me," Cheryl said in disgust.

Angela felt happy with the way the conversation was going, when Miss Berry suddenly said, "Well, I see Angela has some exciting news to share with the class."

"Yes," Angela said quickly. "My mother's on . . ." Angela couldn't remember what it was called. "She's on . . ."

"Maybe you'll think of it later," Miss Berry said gently.

"Well, anyway, she's *not* going to jail," Angela said, and she sat back in her chair.

Miss Berry seemed surprised. She cleared her throat and began to tell the class about the Christmas Drive for the Needy.

"There are people in this world who are far less fortunate than we are," Miss Berry began, "far, far less fortunate. . . ."

Angela was only half-listening. She was trying to remember what her mother was "on."

"No one wants clothes with holes or old broken toys," Miss Berry was saying. "Christmas is a time of giving, and I hope we will all remember those less fortunate."

Angela could not figure out who was going to get the nice toys and clothes they were supposed to bring into school this week.

"I'm not bringing in a thing," Cheryl whispered. "Do you know who really gets that stuff?"

"Who?" Angela asked.

"Poor people," Cheryl told her.

"Oh," Angela said. "Does Miss Berry know?"

"Oh Angela," Cheryl said crossly, "don't be such a baby."

Angela could not figure out what she had said wrong.

Tina's sixth grade class was having a debate about the space program, but Tina was having trouble paying attention.

She kept checking in her pocket to make sure the shopping list and money were still there. She wrote out daily and weekly lists of chores for running the household smoothly.

Once or twice she saw Melissa watching her, but, by now, Tina felt she had more important things to think about.

By the afternoon Tina was working on plans for redecorating the whole apartment while her mother was on jury duty, starting with the bathroom. She wondered if she might buy a set of matching towels. (Tina was sure her family was the only family in the world who didn't even have two towels that were alike.)

She was busy drawing pictures of how she would rearrange the furniture—and even break down a few walls—when the bell rang at the end of the day.

The Invitation

On the way to the supermarket after school, Tina and Angela stopped in at the Bed and Bath Shoppe to price sets of matching towels. They were quite expensive. Angela enjoyed shopping of any kind and the two girls spent a long time looking over the designer sheets and pillowcases, too.

It had stopped raining. The shopping mall was decorated with Christmas wreaths. Christmas songs were playing on the loudspeakers.

Angela sighed. "Isn't that the most beautiful wreath you ever saw, Tina?"

"It's made of plastic," Tina said with disgust.

"That's why it sparkles," Angela said. "It's

much nicer than the other kind. And, oh, Tina! Listen! They're playing 'Rudolph the Red-Nosed Reindeer.' Isn't that your favorite song?"

"Ugh!" Tina said. "It sounds awful. I think the reindeer must be singing it."

Tina was beginning to wonder if she were getting too old for Christmas. Everything seemed so fake. She looked down at Angela and wished she were still young enough to think plastic wreaths were beautiful.

Angela was standing very still, her head cocked to one side.

"No, Tina," she said. "I don't think those are reindeers singing the *words*." She listened to a few more lines of the song. "That might be a reindeer humming in the back—" Angela suddenly looked up at Tina. "Oh no!" she said. "You were only kidding, weren't you?"

Tina burst out laughing. It was fun to have a little sister who believed everything you said.

When they finally got to the supermarket, Tina asked her little sister if she would like to ride in a shopping cart.

"What?" Angela was horrified. "I'm five and a half years old! What if someone from my kindergarten sees me?"

"I just thought it might be faster," Tina said.

"Can I push the cart?" Angela asked. "Oh *please!*"

"I guess so," Tina said.

Angela had another idea. "Um . . . Tina, can I hold the shopping list?" Angela thought how wonderful it would be if someone from Miss Berry's kindergarten class came into the supermarket and saw Angela pushing the shopping cart and reading the shopping list.

"Angela," Tina said, "you can't read."

"I happen to be a Ready-to-Reader," Angela told her sister. "Miss Berry said so." (A Ready-to-Reader knew all the letters of the alphabet and how each one sounded.)

Tina sighed and handed Angela the shopping list. "I'll have to read it to you," she said.

Angela looked at the first item.

"Marshmallows!" Angela said. "It says 'marshmallows'!"

Tina stared at the list. "It *does* say 'marshmallows,' " Tina said. "How did you know that?"

"I told you I was a Ready-to-Reader," Angela said. She did *not* tell Tina that it was the only word she could read. Angela had studied marshmallow packages for years.

Tina was very impressed. "Read the next word," she said to Angela.

The next word started with a "P" so Angela guessed "peas."

"Right!" Tina couldn't get over it. "You can read!" she said. "Wait until I tell Mom!"

Just then Tina heard someone calling her name. She turned around and saw Melissa running towards her.

"Oh Tina!" Melissa shouted. "I'm so glad I found you!"

Tina figured Melissa had gotten over her bad mood.

"Please say you'll go!" Melissa said breathlessly.

"Go where?" Tina asked.

"To the ballet with us tonight. It's *The Nutcracker*—I know you've probably seen it a million times, but it's a benefit."

Tina had not seen *The Nutcracker*, not even once, but she didn't tell Melissa that.

"What's a benefit?" she asked.

"Oh, you know," Melissa said. "It's for poor children or orphans or something."

"Will they be there?" Tina asked.

"Who?" Melissa stared at Tina.

"Well, the poor children—the orphans?"

Melissa laughed very loud. "Don't be ridiculous, Tina," Melissa said. "It's to raise money *for* them. It's very glamorous."

"Oh," Tina said, and she wished she were more sophisticated. Then she remembered.

"Oh, Melissa, I'd really like to go, but, you see, my mother is on jury duty—"

"I just talked to her on the phone," Melissa interrupted. "She got off early and she says you can go."

"On a school night?" Tina asked.

"Don't be ridiculous," Melissa said again.

No one was inviting Angela anyplace so she stopped listening and looked out the window.

Suddenly Angela's heart began to beat very fast. She saw Cheryl White walking past the supermarket window with her mother. The most grown-up girl in Miss Berry's kindergarten was coming in the door!

"Tina!" Angela tugged on the sleeve of her sister's jacket. "I know where the peas are. I know where the marshmallows are, too. I'll go get them."

Tina just nodded and went on talking to Melissa.

Angela pushed the cart up the aisle and hid behind the bread shelves. She peeked around the corner and saw Cheryl and her mother walk over to the line of shopping carts. She watched as Cheryl's mother rejected one shopping cart and pulled out another.

Cheryl climbed into the shopping cart and settled into the little seat. She shoved her bony legs out through the holes in the front.

Angela could not believe her eyes. The most grown-up girl in Miss Berry's kindergarten was going to ride in a shopping cart!

Slowly, Angela pushed her cart out from behind the bread shelves. She bent her head down over the shopping list and pretended to read it. She wanted to time it perfectly. She wanted to pass Cheryl and her mother at exactly the right moment. . . .

The loudspeaker in the supermarket was playing "Frosty the Snowman."

"Tina," Melissa said, "I think I should tell you I invited someone else."

"You mean Sarah is coming?" Tina was relieved. It would be less scary if Sarah came, too.

"Of course not," Melissa said sharply. "Sarah

wouldn't have the faintest idea how to act at a thing like this."

"Who did you invite?" Tina felt very nervous. She was sure she wouldn't know how to act either. She wasn't sure she wanted to go.

"Well." Melissa tossed her long blonde hair out of her eyes. "I told my mother I wouldn't go unless you went, too, and . . . um . . . Nathaniel."

"You asked Nathaniel to go?" Tina asked.

Melissa nodded and looked down at the floor.

"My brother?"

"I just thought it would be convenient," Melissa mumbled. "He said he'd go if you did."

Lately, Tina had noticed that Melissa seemed very interested in her brother. Melissa often asked if she could go to Tina's house after school, but only if she knew Nathaniel was going to be home. Tina didn't mind. She was proud of her brother. She was glad Nathaniel had been invited, too.

"You won't believe where we're going to eat afterwards," Melissa said.

"Where?" Tina asked.

"At the Top of the Stars!"

Tina gasped. "You mean that restaurant that turns? But it's so expensive!"

Melissa shrugged. "Don't worry, Tina," she said. "My parents can afford it."

Cheryl's mother was the fastest shopper Angela had ever seen. As soon as Angela caught up to them at the eggs, Cheryl's mother was on her way to the meat counter. Cheryl hadn't even noticed Angela yet.

Angela decided to try a different tactic. When Cheryl's mother stopped in front of the cheeses, Angela turned her cart around and raced it back up the aisle and down the next one. She was planning to cut them off when they reached the corner.

But when Angela got near the end of that aisle, it was blocked by a shopping cart loaded with groceries. The cart was parked right in the middle of the aisle. There was no room to pass.

Angela stared with dismay at the abandoned cart.

"Who belongs to this?" she called, but there was no one around.

For a brief moment Angela wondered what happened to people who touched other people's carts in the supermarket. But this was an emergency. She had to get through.

Angela left her own cart at the side of the aisle and tried to push the other person's cart out of the way. She looked up and saw that Cheryl was now right at the end of the aisle.

Angela decided to hold on to the cart she was pushing for just a little while longer. It looked so impressive piled high with groceries, and her own cart was still empty. She pushed it to the end of the aisle, right past Cheryl and over to the frozen foods.

Angela heard Cheryl gasp. "I know that girl!" she heard Cheryl say.

Angela blushed and looked down at her list.

"She's in my class!" Cheryl sounded very distressed.

Angela stood on tiptoe and studied the frozen food in the cooler. She picked out a package with a picture of peas on it and placed it on top of the groceries in the cart that belonged to someone else. No. She couldn't do that!

Angela shook her head sadly the way her mother did. "Too 'spensive," she mumbled and she put the frozen peas back.

Suddenly she heard a clatter. Out of the corner of her eye she saw Cheryl trying desperately to climb out of the shopping cart.

"What are you doing?" Cheryl's mother had started shaking the cart, trying to get Cheryl to sit down again.

But Cheryl's foot was caught. She turned and twisted and fell into the back of the shopping cart.

Angela could hear the sound of eggs cracking. She glanced up in time to see Cheryl's mother drive the cart right into a row of soda bottles, which fell on the floor and broke.

"Now look what you made me do!" Cheryl's mother yelled at Cheryl.

Cheryl began to cry. "It's your fault, Mommy. It's all your fault. Angela's mother lets her shop. You don't let me do *anything*!"

Angela was pleased. That was exactly what she had hoped to hear. It was too late to go back and get her own cart, so she tiptoed daintily through the puddle of red soda, pushing the other person's cart in front of her.

She pushed the cart faster and faster until she found Tina. Tina was still talking to Melissa.

Tina smiled when she saw Angela.

"Did you get everything?" Tina asked her. "Angela can read, you know," Tina told Melissa proudly. "She did all the shopping."

Angela stared up at Tina.

"Why don't you wait on line at the check-out counter," Tina suggested. "I'll be right there."

"But . . ." Angela looked down at the groceries in the shopping cart she was pushing. She noticed that the person had bought the same kind of coffee her mother always bought. And there were cans of tuna fish—Angela could tell by the size and the shape. *We always buy tuna fish*, Angela thought. *And hash, too! That's what we eat.*

Angela was delighted. It occurred to her that people probably bought pretty much the same groceries.

On the way to the check-out counter Angela picked up a bag of marshmallows.

Then she stood on line and looked straight ahead. She tried to ignore the confusion in the supermarket. Men in white aprons were running around with broom, mops, and dustpans. Somewhere a little girl was screaming, "You never let me do *anything*!"

The man in front of Angela winked at her.

"Shopping for your mother?" he asked.

Angela nodded. She tried to read the cover of a bride magazine on a rack near the counter, but, unfortunately, the word "marshmallow" wasn't on it.

She could hear a very cross woman telling everyone that someone had emptied out her entire shopping cart, ". . . and I was only gone a minute."

Angela unloaded the groceries onto the counter while Tina said good-bye to Melissa.

Most of the items in the cart looked familiar to Angela. They were the sort of things her mother would buy. But the jars of baby food bothered her.

The clerk began checking out their groceries. Angela looked at Tina. Tina was in a happy daze. She wasn't even looking at the counter. The clerk rang up the order and Tina gave him the two twenty-dollar bills. Then the clerk packed the groceries into large brown shopping bags.

Angela was relieved when all the groceries were in bags.

Tina looked so happy and excited, Angela didn't want to spoil everything by telling her they had just bought someone else's groceries.

The Great
Big Surprise

Nathaniel was waiting for them at the door when they got home.

"I don't get it," he said to Tina. "Why did Melissa invite *me*?"

"I told you, she likes you," Tina said. "Why do you think she laughs so loud at your jokes?"

"Because they're funny?" Nathaniel seemed a little hurt.

"No, because she likes you," Tina said.

"But she's only a sixth-grader," Nathaniel said.

"Sixth-graders can like people," Tina told him.

Nathaniel turned bright red. He didn't seem to know what to say to that.

"Are you sure it's all right if we go?" Tina

asked her mother. She thought her mother looked a little tired.

"Of course. You can't miss something like this!" She sighed. "I don't know why I should be so tired. All I did was sit around the jury room all day. I wasn't even called. They sent us all home early."

"What did you do there?" Tina asked.

"Nothing much. Read the newspaper. Made a friend." Her mother smiled.

Angela was dragging the grocery bags into the kitchen, one by one.

"I'm so proud of you two," their mother said. "Doing all the shopping like this. What a help." She went to change her clothes.

"Tina," Angela said. "Don't tell Mommy I did all the shopping. I want it to be a great big surprise. I'll put all the groceries away. I know where everything goes."

Angela had it all figured out. She would simply hide the jars of baby food, line everything else up neatly on the shelves, and no one would notice a thing.

She put on her mother's apron. Then she decided it would be a good idea to disguise the jars of baby food before putting them away. She ran the hot water and, one by one, put the jars of baby food under the tap. She had seen her mother do this when she wanted to peel labels off jars. Angela did a very good job of peeling off the labels.

Then she climbed onto the counter and hid the jars way at the back of the top shelf.

Now they were just mysterious jars.

Sugar went on the second shelf; so did the coffee.

Marshmallows went in the bread box.

Tuna fish on the first shelf.

There were quite a lot of cans of tuna fish. Angela liked tuna fish and she liked the labels on the cans this woman bought. It was a different brand from the kind her mother usually bought, but Angela had watched enough commercials on television to know that tuna fish came in different brands. Sometimes tuna fish had bumblebees on it; sometimes mermaids, and, in this case, laughing cats. She piled the cans neatly in stacks of threes.

Angela also liked the cans of beef stew and hash with pictures of smiling dogs on them.

Soap flakes under the sink. . . .

Angela took some time to rearrange the cabinet under the sink so it would look neater. She felt very happy.

She sat down to take a rest, eat a marshmallow, and think about the cozy dinner she and her mother would have that evening after her mother found out what a good little helper she was. She was pleased she would have her mother all to herself. She ate another marshmallow and got back to work. . . .

"Are you all right in there?" Her mother was knocking on the kitchen door.

Angela called, "I'm almost finished, Mommy. Are you all ready for the great big surprise?"

"First come out and see how nice your brother and sister look," her mother called.

Angela went into the hall.

"Oh, Tina," Angela breathed. "Your hair is so fluffy!"

"Too fluffy?" Tina asked, patting it nervously.

"No, it's beautiful!" Angela told her.

Tina was wearing a black velvet jumper and a lacy white blouse. Nathaniel looked handsome in his blue blazer and red tie. They were both carrying the ski jackets they wore every day.

"I guess those jackets will just have to do."

Their mother sighed. "No one will notice when you get inside."

"Oh, Mom," Tina said. "I forgot to give you the money left over from the groceries."

"That's all right," her mother said. "It can't be much. Keep it just in case."

When they were gone, Angela told her mother to close her eyes. She took her mother's hand and led her into the kitchen.

"No peeking," Angela said. She climbed onto the chair and opened the cupboard doors. "Now you can look."

Her mother opened her eyes and gasped. "It's so beautiful!" she said. "Everything is so neat!"

"And guess who did all the shopping," Angela said. "Guess, Mommy, guess."

Her mother was still staring at the cans in the cupboard. She picked one up and looked at it. Then she put it back. She looked puzzled.

"Okay," Angela said. "I'll give you a hint. It wasn't Tina. Now guess who did the shopping."

"Someone with a dog and a cat?" her mother asked.

"No, Mommy!" Angela did not think that was a very good guess. "I did the shopping. I did it all by myself!"

"Oh, really?" her mother said, but not in a surprised voice. She went to the refrigerator and looked inside. She closed the door. Then she went to the kitchen table and sat down.

Angela was worried. Her mother was staring blankly at the wall.

"Is something missing?" Angela asked.

"Yes, Angela," her mother said quietly. "The food is missing. Tina just went off with all my money. Naturally the bank is closed. There is no food in the house. Wait a minute. Let me rephrase that. There *is* food in the house. There is food for dogs and cats. Strangely enough, we do not have a dog or a cat. We do not have any pets. Have you noticed any pets running around our house?"

Angela blinked and shook her head.

"Now, Angela," her mother said in that same quiet voice. "Let's start at the beginning. What exactly happened at the supermarket this afternoon?"

"Are you going to yell?" Angela whispered.

"Probably," her mother said.

"Good," Angela said. Anything was better than that quiet voice. It really scared her. She began her story. . . .

"I see," her mother said. "You stole someone else's shopping cart. . . ."

"Borrowed," Angela said. "I borrowed it."

"And Tina stood there like an idiot and paid for everything," her mother said.

"Tina's not an idiot," Angela mumbled. "Don't call her an idiot. She was just happy."

It was a great relief when her mother finally started yelling.

The Nutcracker

Tina and Nathaniel stood under a big crystal chandelier in the theater lobby and waited for the ballet to begin. They had both seen the poster on the wall. It was a picture of a skinny boy with sunken cheeks. "DO YOU KNOW WHAT IT MEANS TO BE HUNGRY?" the poster said.

"How can people let kids suffer like that?" Nathaniel whispered to Tina.

"Well, at least the people here are trying to do something about it," Tina whispered back. "I hope they make a million dollars tonight."

Melissa was on the other side of the lobby, talking to a girl she knew from camp.

Melissa's mother glided over to Tina and Nathaniel. Tina thought she looked beautiful. Mrs. Glenn was wearing a white knit dress and simple gold jewelry. She took them each by the arm and led them through the crowd of people in fur coats. Tina and Nathaniel bunched their ski jackets into tight little balls and tried to keep them out of sight.

"I'd like you to meet two of Melissa's little friends," she said to a woman with blonde stripes in her hair. "They're the children of Richard Steele—you know—the cellist."

Tina and Nathaniel looked at each other. Their father wasn't famous. He played the cello in the city orchestra. His name wasn't even on the program.

The woman with striped hair looked blank for a moment. Then she nodded as if she had heard of Richard Steele the cellist—as if everybody had.

"How delightful," she said. "And how *is* your father?"

"He's away on a concert tour," Tina said politely. She knew perfectly well the woman was only pretending, but her father *was* away on a concert tour and Tina knew it sounded good.

"Of course," the woman murmured.

Mr. Glenn came over and put his arm around Nathaniel's shoulder. "Well, my boy. How would you like to meet a friend of mine?" He whispered loudly in Nathaniel's ear, "You may be interested to know that he drives a Ferrari."

"Wow!" Nathaniel said. His main interest nowadays was sports cars, "but not the cheap kind," he told everyone. "Sure, I'd like to meet him."

Tina was pleased her brother knew so much about sports cars. Mr. Glenn had a Porsche and liked sports cars, too. He said Nathaniel was a boy after his own heart.

Tina watched them walk away together. She thought Mr. Glenn was very brave to wear red pants and a gold jacket with horses all over it. Most of the other men wore dark suits.

She walked over to a table covered with pamphlets. The benefit was for an organization called Rescue the Children.

"Can I take some home?" Tina asked the woman sitting behind the table. The woman was wearing a sweater and a skirt. Tina thought she had a very kind face.

"Of course," the woman said. "Would you like one of our Rescue the Children posters?"

Tina nodded and watched the woman take a poster out of a box and lay it on the table. THERE WILL BE NO CHRISTMAS FOR THERESA, the big lettering on the poster said. Tina thought the little girl on the poster looked like Angela. She had big dark eyes and short dark hair. Tina had a lump in her throat.

"Are you on our mailing list?" the woman asked her.

Tina shook her head and tried to swallow the lump in her throat.

"Would you like to be?"

Tina nodded and gave the woman her address.

Then she suddenly realized what it meant to be on a mailing list. They would expect her to contribute a lot of money.

"Wait a minute," she said to the woman. "My family doesn't . . . um . . . have any extra money. I mean, you'd just be wasting stamps on us. We aren't poor exactly, but, at the end of the month, after the bills are paid, my mother says . . ."

Tina bit her lip and looked at the floor. She couldn't figure out why she was telling the woman all this. "You see, my mother happens to be against hunger, too. She writes a lot of letters to the mayor about the hungry homeless people in the city. But, you see, she doesn't even have a mink coat. She has a plaid coat and wears this old hat with a pom pom on the top. . . ."

Tina decided it was time for her to get to the point.

"I really want to help," Tina said, "more than anything, but, you see, I don't really belong here. I just came with my friend Melissa."

"Of course you belong here," the woman said, somewhat sharply. "People who care belong here. Caring is the most important part."

Tina thought that was a very nice thing to say, but she felt desperate.

"Caring doesn't help these children get food," Tina said. Tears were stinging her eyes.

The woman looked at her thoughtfully. "Caring hurts, doesn't it?" she asked softly.

"I wish I could do something about it right now," Tina said. "Right this minute."

The woman rolled up the poster and handed it to Tina. "Right now," she said, "your job is to enjoy this ballet. Being miserable doesn't help anyone. Later on, I'm sure you'll think of some way to help."

"Thank you." Tina felt much better. She tucked the poster under her arm. "I'll put it on

44

my wall as soon as I get home," she promised.

The ballet was beautiful. Melissa sat between Tina and Nathaniel. At first Tina was embarrassed when her brother kept saying things like, "Wow! Did you see that guy jump? Wasn't it amazing?" Then he'd applaud very loudly— even if no one else in the audience was applauding. But, after a while, Tina noticed that Melissa had started applauding to keep Nathaniel company.

When the Christmas tree on the stage suddenly grew into a giant tree and the dolls came to life, Tina got tingles up and down her neck. "Christmas *is* magic," she told herself.

After the ballet, Mr. Glenn and Nathaniel went to get the car, which was parked in a garage a few blocks away.

Tina, Melissa, and Mrs. Glenn waited for them by the fountain in front of the theater. It had gotten very cold. Melissa buttoned up the top button of her red coat with the black velvet collar. Mrs. Glenn huddled under the hood of her mink coat and Tina zipped up her blue ski jacket.

Not more than a few feet away from where they were standing, Tina saw a man picking through a garbage pail.

At first Tina thought he had lost something. Then she saw the man bend down and pull out a box of Uncle Freddy's Fried Chicken. He shook the box. It was empty. Tina looked at Melissa and her mother, but they didn't seem to see the man. Tina tried not to see him either.

Tina was relieved when, just at that moment, Mr. Glenn and Nathaniel drove up. She hoped the man didn't see her get into such a fancy car.

"Well, young man," Mr. Glenn said to Nathaniel. "You must be mighty hungry."

"I *am* hungry," Nathaniel said.

"I'm starving," said Melissa.

"Please don't say that!" Tina burst out.

Everyone laughed except Nathaniel.

Tina's stomach was rumbling. She hadn't had anything to eat since lunchtime, but she was no longer looking forward to dining at the Top of the Stars.

It no longer seemed like fun. It didn't seem right. In fact, it didn't seem fair to be eating dinner at all.

"Mommy," Angela said shyly. "Please promise. Please promise me you won't tell anyone I ate banana and egg yolk."

"Well, I'm not sure it *is* banana and egg yolk," her mother said, "especially since there is no label on the jar. That was just a guess."

Now that the yelling was over, Angela and her mother were making the best of things. They were having a cozy dinner for two with five unmarked jars of baby food sitting in front of them on the kitchen table.

They had decided not to eat anything that was either orange or green.

"There's nothing to be embarrassed about," her mother said. "After all, I'm eating baby food, too." She took a spoonful out of one of the jars. "These pears aren't half bad. I always thought the pears were pretty good."

"You've eaten baby food before?" Angela gasped and stared at her mother.

"When you were little," her mother said, and she cleared the jars away.

She sat down again and studied Angela with amusement. "You know, Angela," she said after a while, "this is not the first time you've ever gone on an illegal shopping expedition."

"What do you mean?" Angela asked her.

Her mother told her about the time she got

lost in a department store. "It was when you were very little," her mother said, "and, of course, you didn't think you were lost. You said you had some shopping to do and you disappeared."

Her mother was laughing. Angela laughed, too, and wished she could remember it.

"You were so cute," her mother said. "You're still cute."

"No, I'm not," Angela said. "I'm too old to be cute." But she was glad her mother still thought so.

"Well, at least Tina and Nathaniel will be eating something fancy tonight. I wonder what they will order at Top of the Stars," her mother said.

"Something grown-up, I guess," Angela said. "Maybe liver."

Among the Stars

Nathaniel opened the red menu with the gold tassel swinging from it. Tina was watching him carefully. She had already read the menu.

"Yikes!" Nathaniel squeaked. "Look at these prices! Ouch! Tina, don't kick me."

Melissa giggled. "These prices aren't so bad," she said. "I'm going to have the shrimp cocktail and steak."

Mrs. Glenn looked as if she were very disappointed in Melissa. "Oh, Melissa," she said. "You always have the same thing. Why don't you try something different for a change?"

"Steak sounds good to me," Mr. Glenn said. "I'm sure the young man will have steak, too."

"I will?" Nathaniel asked. "But it costs—"

"You're a growing boy." Mr. Glenn laughed. "What about you, Tina?"

"I *think* I know what I want," Tina said.

Tina had already decided to have the least expensive thing on the menu. She didn't think she could get away with just ordering an appetizer or soup. That probably wasn't even allowed in a restaurant like this. The least expensive item cost $18.50. Tina had never heard of it before, but it was listed under Seafood, and Tina liked fish.

She gazed out the window at the view. The restaurant turned very slowly, so slowly you couldn't really feel it turn, but the view kept changing ever so slightly. She could see the lights from the harbor bridge way below and the stars overhead.

"Such a perfect night," Mrs. Glenn sighed. "It's so clear."

Tina thought how nice it would be if, while they were turning way up here among the stars, the world below them changed. How nice it would be if it became a different planet—a planet where everyone had enough to eat. She said a silent prayer. . . .

"It's your turn, Tina," Mr. Glenn said.

Tina looked up and saw the waiter standing next to her.

"Mademoiselle?" The waiter bowed to her.

Tina opened the menu. "I'll have the—" She caught herself. She had almost said, "I'll have the $18.50"!

Since she didn't know how to pronounce the fish she wanted, she pointed to it.

"*Anguilles*?" The waiter's eyebrows went up. "*Anguilles au vert*?"

Tina nodded.

Mrs. Glenn gasped. "Oh, Tina, are you sure? It's such a . . . a *cultivated* taste!"

"I always order that when I go to restaurants," Tina said. "It's my favorite."

Nathaniel was staring at her with his mouth open. Tina was afraid he was going to say something, so she gave him another kick to keep him quiet. This time it was a very gentle kick. Nathaniel closed his mouth abruptly.

The waiter was smiling at Tina with approval and admiration. Mrs. Glenn was looking at her the same way. Tina was glad she had ordered *anguilles*—whatever that was.

"You know," Mrs. Glenn said, "I adore *anguilles* myself, but tonight I had my heart set on the duck à l'orange." She nodded to the waiter.

The waiter wrote their orders down, picked up their menus, and left.

"Did you hear what Tina is having, Melissa?" Mrs. Glenn gave her daughter a very disapproving look. "Tina is having *anguilles*."

"Never heard of it," Melissa grumbled, "and I don't really care."

Mrs. Glenn turned to her husband. "Remember, darling, we had *anguilles* in the south of France."

"I certainly *do* remember." Mr. Glenn shuddered. "I can't say I was crazy about it either. I guess eel just isn't my cup of tea."

EEL? Tina felt as if the restaurant had just come to a lurching halt and was beginning to spin around upside down. She had ordered eel!

"Oh, Tina!" Melissa said. "How *could* you?"

"I like eel," Tina murmured, but she wanted to scream.

It took a long time for the food to arrive. During this time Tina was saying a different prayer. She was praying that the waiter would suddenly appear and announce that he was terribly sorry, they had just run out of eels and what would Tina like instead?

When the waiter finally brought the main course, he carelessly tossed the plates of steak in front of Nathaniel, Melissa, and Mr. Glenn. He dumped the duck à l'orange in front of Mrs. Glenn. But Tina's plate of cut-up eel he laid down very gently. *"Bon appetit,"* he whispered. But he spoke only to Tina.

Tina looked questioningly at Mrs. Glenn.

"He said, 'Enjoy your meal,' " Mrs. Glenn explained with a smile.

"Merci beaucoup," Tina said to the waiter. She was happy she knew how to say 'thank you' in French.

The waiter stood there for a moment looking fondly at Tina. Then he said to Mrs. Glenn, *"Elle est mignonne."*

After he had gone away, Mrs. Glenn explained that it was almost impossible to translate that expression, but the waiter had meant that Tina was a very sweet and fine little girl.

Tina looked down at the plate of cut-up eel covered with green sauce and knew she was going to eat it—every last bit of it. She couldn't let the waiter down; she felt she owed it to him. And, somehow, she felt she owed it to the world.

When Nathaniel offered Tina a bite of his

steak, she shook her head at him. Then she took a deep breath.

The first bite was the hardest. Tina had to give herself a lecture first: "Tina," she told herself firmly, "eels are just another fish; eels are not snakes. If eels were snakes, they would *not* have been listed under Seafood on the menu; they would have been listed under Snakes. . . ."

That didn't seem to help, so she tried something else. She thought about the people in the world who were going to bed hungry or waking up hungry in places where the sun was now rising. . . .

With freezing cold hands, Tina picked up her fork and knife. She cut a piece of eel and covered it with lots of green sauce. She put it in her mouth, chewed it, and swallowed.

Nathaniel was watching her. Tina knew her brother had never been so proud of her as he was at that moment.

Tina smiled at him and cut another piece.

She had survived!

Coming Down from the Stars

During the ride home, Mrs. Glenn asked Tina and Nathaniel if their mother was involved in any charity work.

"She's very interested in good causes," Tina said quickly, and she wondered if she could count jury duty as a good cause.

"Oh really?" Mrs. Glenn said. "Which ones?"

Tina didn't want to say her mother wrote letters all the time, so she tried to think of a fancier way of putting it.

"She's . . . um . . . in touch with the mayor's office. . . ." Tina began.

"She writes letters all the time," Nathaniel said, "about shelters for the homeless."

Tina thought about the man she had just seen shaking the box of fried chicken and wondered where he slept at night. All at once she felt very proud of her mother.

"Your mother sounds like a very concerned human being," Mrs. Glenn said.

"Oh, she is," Tina said. "Very."

"I wonder if she would be interested in our Rescue the Children Program," Mrs. Glenn said.

"I have a poster right here about that," Tina said. "A lady gave it to me, but I don't know much about what they do."

"Well, it's simply marvelous," Mrs. Glenn told them. "You see, for only seventeen dollars a month a family can sponsor a child—help provide food, medical care, clothing—"

"But you don't have to change their diapers," Mr. Glenn said, and he laughed.

"The family who adopts the child in this way gets letters about the child's progress and often letters from the child, too," Mrs. Glenn explained.

"Really?" Tina couldn't believe it. "That's fantastic. Seventeen dollars a month doesn't sound like much."

"It's not much when you know you might be saving a life," Mrs. Glenn said.

"What a terrific deal!" Nathaniel was very enthusiastic. "I'll bet Mom would be interested."

Mrs. Glenn smiled at him. "We have adopted two orphans ourselves," she said.

"You never told me that, Melissa," Tina said, but Melissa just shrugged. She did not seem to be enjoying the conversation.

"Why don't I bring some material on the program when I come to your school on Wednesday to help with the Christmas Drive?"

"Oh no!" Melissa wailed. "You're not coming to my school."

"Of course I am, Melissa," Mrs. Glenn said. "You know perfectly well I always help with the Drive. You did get a notice about it, didn't you, Tina?"

"Um . . . yes," Tina said, but she didn't want to hear about the Christmas Drive for the Needy. Her school had that every year. She wanted to hear about the Rescue the Children Program. It sounded so important and exciting. Tina figured that, if her family signed up right away, they might be able to rescue a child in time for Christmas!

Tina felt in her jacket pocket. The money left over from the groceries was still there. Maybe she could give Mrs. Glenn a small deposit—a sort of down payment—so they could sign up right away. She counted the money. To her surprise, there was more than seventeen dollars left over from the groceries!

"Here," she said suddenly to Mrs. Glenn. "Here's the money for the first month. We want to rescue a child right now—starting tonight."

Mrs. Glenn was surprised. "Well, dear," she said, "that's very sweet of you, but it would be better if you asked your mother first. You know, you commit yourself to supporting a child for one whole year."

"Oh, please take it now so we can start right away," Tina begged her. "I'm absolutely positive it will be all right with Mom."

"Well. . . ." Mrs. Glenn was hesitant. "Hold onto it until Wednesday. You can meet me outside the school cafeteria at lunchtime. I'll give you the forms to fill out. In any case, I'm sure your mother will want to write a check instead. It's tax deductible, of course."

"What's that mean?" Tina asked.

"It means we pay less taxes," Nathaniel told her.

Tina reluctantly put the money back into her

pocket. "I'll bring the check on Wednesday," she promised Mrs. Glenn.

On the way up in the elevator, Nathaniel said, "Where did you get all that money?"

"Left over from the groceries," Tina said. "Remember, Mom said we could use it if we needed it."

She sighed. "Oh, Nathaniel, won't Mom be excited? Do you know what she's probably going to say?"

"No, what is she going to say?"

"She's going to say that with the money we save on taxes, we should get two orphans. . . ."

But their mother didn't say anything at all. She was fast asleep when they got home.

Before they went to bed, Nathaniel went into the kitchen to get a snack.

"You're still hungry?" Tina called after him.

A few seconds later she heard him screech. She went into the kitchen to find out what was going on.

"I knew it!" Nathaniel kept saying over and over. He seemed very excited. "I just knew they would get us a dog for Christmas!"

Tina stared at the carton on the kitchen table, full of dog food. . . .

". . . and cat food, too," Tina said. "We can't be getting a dog *and* a cat," but she thought it was about time. They had never had a pet.

Then she saw the note on the table.

Dear Tina —

I hope you had a lovely time.

Please return this box of groceries to the supermarket after school tomorrow and see if you can get credit. There is nothing in the house so you'll have to use part of the money you have to take Angela out for breakfast. Please give Nathaniel some money and leave me a few dollars to get down to the courthouse tomorrow morning. I have to go very early.

Angela made me promise not to yell at you, but please don't let her do the shopping again — not for a few years, anyway.

    Love.

      Mom

"Angela can't read," Tina said.

"I don't get it," Nathaniel said. "Are we getting a dog or aren't we?" He looked at Tina's face. "What's the matter?" he asked Tina.

Tina felt sick. "The money I have in my pocket isn't extra money at all. We need it."

Then she went and got a pad and paper. She sat down at the kitchen table and started to write down numbers.

"What are you doing?" Nathaniel asked.

"It can't be that much," Tina said to herself. "I must have multiplied wrong."

A minute later she turned around.

"Nathaniel," she said in a shaky voice, "do you realize that seventeen dollars a month is the same as two hundred and four dollars a year?"

"It does sound like a lot when you put it that way," Nathaniel admitted.

"Two hundred and four dollars!" Tina was frightened. "Mommy and Daddy don't have two hundred and four extra dollars. Let's face it, Nathaniel," Tina said flatly. "We can't afford to rescue a child."

Angela Meets Theresa

On Tuesday morning Angela woke up and went to see if Tina was up yet.

The door to Tina's room was halfway open. Angela peeked inside. To her surprise she saw that Tina was already dressed.

Angela watched as Tina climbed up on a chair and carefully removed the big poster that was hanging on her wall.

It was a poster called "Puppy Among the Pansies." Tina had had it on her wall for two years, and Angela always enjoyed looking at it. The puppy in the picture was brownish-red, and he matched one of the pansies perfectly. He had big floppy ears.

"Oh Tina!" Angela burst out. "Why are you taking it down? Don't you want it anymore?"

Tina turned around and almost fell off the chair.

"Oh, can I have it?" Angela begged her sister. "Can I have 'Puppy Among the Pansies' for my room?"

Tina took the poster down and folded it.

"I'll be your best friend," Angela said. She held her breath and waited for Tina to say something.

"Here." Tina handed Angela the poster. "I guess I'm finished with it."

"I'll put it up right now," Angela said. "Can I borrow the Scotch tape?"

"Let me finish using it first," Tina told her.

Angela watched Tina put up her new poster. She didn't think it was a very nice poster compared to "Puppy Among the Pansies." It wasn't even in color. It was a photograph of a girl with big dark eyes standing in a tumbledown doorway. She wasn't even wearing shoes, and she looked very unhappy. Angela thought Tina's taste in posters had gone downhill.

It was a good thing Tina had used the Scotch tape first. Angela used up the rest of the roll trying to get the puppy poster to stick to the wall in her room. There was Scotch tape all over the place, but she finally got the poster to stay up. Angela stood back to admire it for a few minutes. Then she went back to Tina's room. Tina was sitting on her bed.

"Where did you get that?" Angela pointed to the poster.

"At the benefit," Tina said. She opened a pamphlet and began to read it.

"Did you have fun?" Angela asked.

" 'Fun' isn't exactly the right word," Tina said crossly.

Angela tried to think of the right word. "Um . . . did you have a good time, Tina?" she asked, but Tina didn't answer. She was too busy reading.

Angela stared into the eyes of the little girl on the poster.

"What does the poster say?" she asked Tina.

"Do you really want to know?" Tina asked.

Angela nodded.

Tina stood up and went over to the poster.

" 'There will be no Christmas for Theresa . . .' " Tina began.

Angela's eyes opened wide. "She was bad— right?" Angela asked.

"No, Angela." Tina was talking in her try-to-be-patient-with-Angela voice. "She was not bad. Listen to the rest. . . ." She went on. Angela could not understand why her sister's voice sounded so funny. It was all choked up.

" '. . . Theresa has never had a stuffed animal. No one has ever given her a present. She has never known a mother's love.' " Tina stopped to control her voice. Then she went on.

" 'Two years ago, Theresa lost her baby brother—' "

Angela interrupted. "Well, that was bad," Angela said. "That was very naughty."

"What was naughty?" Tina seemed surprised.

"Losing her baby brother," Angela said. "If I had a baby brother, I would always make sure I knew where he was."

"Oh honestly, Angela!" Tina exploded. Angela was frightened. "They mean her baby brother died!"

"Oh!" Angela said, and she felt sad—very, very sad.

"What did he die of?" she whispered.

"He got sick," Tina said. "The family couldn't afford medicine for him." She sat on the edge of her bed and began to cry.

Angela said, "Tina, don't cry. Please don't cry." She put her arms around her sister.

Angela hardly ever cried herself. She was always impressed with how many tears came out of her sister's eyes.

"Don't you see," Tina sobbed, "even if we *could* afford to rescue one or two children, there are thousands more like her." Tina pointed to Theresa.

"More children who don't have stuffed animals?" Angela asked in horror.

"Oh honestly, Angela," Tina said. "That's not the most serious part."

It sounded pretty serious to Angela.

Angela hugged her sister while her sister wept.

"I hate the world," Tina said over and over.

"Please don't hate the world," Angela begged her. "There are nice things."

"Name me one nice thing," Tina said angrily.

Angela stroked Tina's hair and tried to think of a very nice thing.

"Christmas!" Angela said. "What about Christmas? It's almost here!"

"I hate Christmas," Tina sobbed. "All it is, is people throwing presents at each other, stuffing themselves with turkey, and cutting down inno-cent Christmas trees. Christmas is *disgusting!*"

Angela was shocked. "Tina," she said. "I don't think you're allowed to say things like that."

"Besides," Tina went on, "if Theresa can't have Christmas, no one should. It should be canceled."

"Can we have it the next day?" Angela asked sadly.

"Oh honestly, Angela!"

On the way to school they stopped at a coffee shop for breakfast. When Angela asked if she could have a second doughnut, Tina said, "You know, Angela, money doesn't grow on trees."

"I know *that*," Angela said. "You get it at the bank," but Tina wasn't listening.

All that morning at school, Angela thought about Theresa. During free play, she went to the art table in her kindergarten and drew a picture of Theresa. She took a green Magic Marker and drew a nice Christmas tree right next to Theresa.

"Little red balls . . ." she whispered to herself, and she drew little red balls on the tree.

". . . and presents," she told herself. "Millions

of presents." Angela drew a big pile of Christmas packages tied with bows under the Christmas tree.

She looked up and saw that Cheryl was sitting across from her, watching her.

"Were you in the supermarket yesterday?" Cheryl asked her.

Angela was delighted, but she said in a casual way, "Yes, I was shopping for my mother."

"Well, I didn't see you," Cheryl said. She paused and stared right at Angela. "I didn't see you *because I wasn't there.*"

Angela stared right back at Cheryl, but she didn't call her a big fat liar. Good citizens did not use words like that. Then she picked up a black Magic Marker and drew some nice party shoes on Theresa's feet.

A few minutes later, she heard Cheryl calling, "Miss Berry! Miss Berry!" Cheryl was standing at Miss Berry's desk. "There's only one strawberry sticker left." She pointed to the box of smelly stickers on the desk. "Can I have it if I am a good citizen this week?"

"Well, Cheryl. . . ." Miss Berry seemed a little unsure of what to say.

"It's mine!" Angela yelled. She rushed across

the room to defend her rights. "I *have* to get strawberry. I have a collection!"

"Now, Angela," Miss Berry said, "Cheryl has never gotten strawberry. I think it would be more generous of you to let Cheryl have it this week."

Angela had no intention of being generous to a big fat liar.

"Come now," Miss Berry said. "We have some nice flower stickers, pizza stickers, bubble gum stickers, and . . . look, Angela! Look at these cute skunk stickers."

Angela stared at Miss Berry in disbelief. Nobody ever wanted skunk stickers. The skunks had flowers behind their ears. When you scratched them, they smelled of perfume; they did not even smell like skunks!

Angela shook her head hard.

"I'm sorry, Angela," Miss Berry said, "but you'll have to pick something else. What about this new sticker? It's a car that smells like gasoline!"

"No!" Angela was almost shouting.

"Can I see that car?" Eddie Bishop came running over to Miss Berry's desk. "Does it really smell like gasoline?"

Cheryl laughed. "Miss Berry, tell Eddie that only good citizens can get smelly stickers."

"Anyone can be a good citizen, Cheryl," Miss Berry said sharply.

"Not me," Eddie said sadly. "I never got one smelly sticker in my whole life."

"If I can't get strawberry, I don't care anymore," Angela said.

"Think it over, Angela," Miss Berry said, and she went to see why there was so much noise in the home corner.

Angela and Eddie stood there for a while looking into the box of smelly stickers.

"Eddie," Angela finally said, "are you thinking about throwing any blocks today?"

Angela had thought it over as Miss Berry had asked her to. She had decided there was no longer any reason to be a good citizen.

And, of all the bad things Eddie did each day, throwing blocks seemed to her the most interesting.

"Don't you usually throw them during free play?" Angela asked politely. She did not want to throw blocks alone—not the first time anyway.

"I sure would like one of those car stickers."

Eddie was still staring down into the box.

Angela looked at him. Eddie had never been interested in those stickers before. She knew he didn't have a chance of getting one. She suddenly thought of something much naughtier than throwing blocks around.

"Look, Eddie," she whispered. "How about this: I be a good citizen for the whole week. Then on Friday I'll ask for the car sticker . . . and give it to you!"

Angela was sure you weren't allowed to give your smelly sticker to someone else. And how wicked it would be to give it to the baddest citizen in the class! Angela was delighted with the idea. She would be tricking Miss Berry. Miss Berry deserved to be tricked.

Eddie did not believe Angela would actually do such a thing, but he followed her around for the rest of the morning to make sure she was being good. And he watched her carefully all afternoon.

Angela was being extra good that day. She was being extra good to punish Miss Berry for giving her strawberry sticker away.

Charity
Begins at Home

Tina sat in class all afternoon trying to write a letter to Mrs. Glenn. She figured it would be less embarrassing than telling her in person when she came to school on Wednesday.

Her sixth-grade teacher kept looking at her. Mr. Glaser was quite young. Tina thought he was extremely good-looking. A few of the girls in the class had crushes on him and had formed a secret club (which everyone knew about) called the I.L.M.G. Club. Tina thought the I Love Mr. Glaser Club was very silly, but she liked Mr. Glaser and thought he was a very interesting teacher. Usually she paid careful attention to everything he said.

But it took her the whole afternoon to get the first line of her letter to Mrs. Glenn.

Dear Mrs. Glenn,
We are sorry to say our family is not in a position to sponsor a child.

"That certainly sounds better than saying we are too poor," Tina told herself. Then she looked up and saw Mr. Glaser watching her with a puzzled expression on his face.

He stopped her in the hall after school.

"Tina." Mr. Glaser looked worried. "Is anything wrong?"

"What?" Tina asked.

"Well, I just wondered. You haven't seemed to be concentrating for the last two days." He seemed a little awkward. "I . . . er . . . just wondered if everything was all right at home."

"Oh, it's fine," Tina said brightly. "Just fine!"

When Tina and Angela got home, their mother was still at the courthouse. Angela took out her picture of Theresa and the Christmas tree and showed it to Tina.

"It's nice, isn't it?" Angela said happily. "And

guess what! Every one of those presents has a stuffed animal in it — all for Theresa!"

"Very funny," Tina said, and she stormed off to her room.

Angela went to her room, too, and closed the door. She took out all her stuffed animals and put them on her bed. Then she curled up with Stuffed Elephant and stared at the wall.

When Nathaniel got home from school, Tina read him the first line of her letter to Mrs. Glenn.

"Dear Mrs. Glenn," she read. "We are sorry to say our family is not in a position to sponsor a child. . . ."

"Tina," Nathaniel said. "Aren't we giving up too easily? Maybe we could find some way to get the money."

"Two hundred and four dollars?" Tina asked him.

"Maybe I could get a job — babysitting or something," Nathaniel said.

"Who would hire you?" Tina asked.

"I've babysat before," Nathaniel said.

"Once," Tina said, "for that kid on the fifth floor. In the afternoon. For two hours. Look, Nathaniel, even if I get a job, too, feeding someone's fish or something, we can't count on the money.

We don't know how much we'll make."

"Then we'll save up and get an orphan next year."

"Next year?" Tina stared at Nathaniel. "Next year doesn't count. I want an orphan *right now!*" and she started to cry.

"Don't be such a baby, Tina," Nathaniel said.

"I'm not a baby," Tina sobbed. "Oh, what am I going to tell Melissa's mother?"

"Is that all you're worried about?" Nathaniel asked.

"No!" Tina shouted. "I want to save a child because I happen to care about other people."

"You're just feeling sorry for yourself," Nathaniel said.

Tina returned the groceries Angela had bought and did the shopping. Then she spent the rest of the afternoon sitting in the living room surrounded by the old clothes her mother had put aside for the Christmas Drive.

"What are you doing with the scissors?" Nathaniel asked.

"What do you think I'm doing?" Tina said crossly. "I'm cutting out the name-tapes, of course. Those are *our* names, Nathaniel. Do you want anyone to know our family contributed such ratty-looking clothes?"

"They don't look so terrible," Nathaniel said.

Tina stopped and looked at him. "Do you know what Melissa brought into the Drive last year? Five boxes of brand-new sweaters. From her father's factory. Mr. Glenn is in the sweater business."

Nathaniel just shrugged. "I'm going to do the laundry now," he said.

Tina put the clothes into a big green plastic bag. Then she got an idea. She went to the hall closet and got her brown rubber boots. She put them in the plastic bag with the clothes for the Drive.

"I'm getting new ones anyway," she told herself. Then she searched through the house for other things to give to the Drive.

She knocked on Angela's door. There was no answer. Tina opened the door and looked in. Angela was lying in her bed, but her eyes were wide open. She didn't say anything to Tina.

"By the way, Angela," Tina said, "did you know our school has a Christmas Drive for the Needy every year?"

"Miss Berry told us," Angela mumbled.

"Maybe you have some toys you don't need," Tina suggested. "Wouldn't you like to contribute something to the Drive?"

"No," Angela said flatly.

"Come on, Angela." Tina was getting annoyed. "You have a million toys. You don't even play with half of them anymore."

"I need them," Angela said.

"I suppose you need every single toy in this room," Tina said. "Aren't you getting a little old for all these stuffed animals?"

Suddenly Tina grabbed a small teddy bear.

"What about this teddy bear?" Tina asked. "It used to belong to me, you know. I'm giving it to the Drive."

"You can't!" Angela sat up quickly. "That's Stuffed Elephant's teddy bear. It belongs to him now!"

"Take it then!" Tina told Stuffed Elephant and she threw the teddy bear.

The teddy bear hit Stuffed Elephant right between the eyes. Tina saw Angela's look of horror, and suddenly felt ashamed of herself. She didn't mean to be throwing bears at stuffed elephants.

Tina decided a lecture would be more dignified. She began it in a cold voice.

"Angela Steele, you happen to be a very lucky little kid. Unfortunately, you also happen to be a spoiled little brat. And do you want to know something? I bought a Christmas present for you, but I am not sure I'm going to give it to you. Do you want to know what it is?"

"Go away, Tina," Angela said.

"It's an album for your strawberry smelly stickers!" Tina said triumphantly.

Tina knew Angela hardly ever cried, but she felt sure her lecture was making an impression on her little sister. Angela was sitting very still, blinking her eyes at Tina.

When Nathaniel came back from the laundry, he passed Angela's room and saw her sitting stiffly on her bed. He went in and sat down next to her. She didn't say anything for a while. She didn't look at Nathaniel. Finally she whispered, "Tina called me a spoiled little brat."

"Look, Angela," Nathaniel said. "Tina's in a bad mood. She's just disappointed that we might not be able to adopt an orphan for Christmas."

"Huh?" Angela looked up at Nathaniel.

Nathaniel tried to explain the Rescue the Children Program to Angela. Angela found it difficult to understand how you could adopt an orphan who didn't even come to live at your house. But she found the idea of getting letters from the orphan quite interesting.

"Can we adopt Theresa?" Angela asked.

"I don't think we get to choose the orphan we want," Nathaniel said.

"I only want Theresa," Angela told him.

"It would be someone *like* Theresa," Nathaniel said, "someone who needs our help just as much as Theresa does."

Angela thought about that.

"Maybe we could get a baby," Angela said. "An orphan baby might be nice." She wondered how it would feel to be someone's big sister for a change. But that made her think about Tina again.

"Just because I don't cry all over the place doesn't mean I don't feel sad about Theresa, too," Angela said.

Nathaniel was quiet for a moment. Then he said, "You hardly ever cry, do you, Angela?" He seemed surprised at the thought. "Sometimes, you know, crying makes people feel better."

"Not me!" Angela's cheeks felt hot. Her heart ached so much she could hardly breathe. "Would

I have to share the orphan with Tina?" she asked.

"Well, of course," Nathaniel said. "The whole family would have to share."

"Then I don't want one," Angela said angrily. "I don't want to share with Tina. If I can't get my own orphan, I don't want one at all," she said . . .

. . . and she hoped Tina wouldn't get one either!

After dinner that evening, Angela told everyone she was going to bed early. She lay in her little room and listened to Tina, Nathaniel, and her mother talking quietly in the kitchen.

"One big happy family except for me," she told her stuffed elephant, who just looked at her with his wise blue eyes.

Angela tried to put herself to sleep by counting sheep jumping rope. She started in the usual way: She lined up the sheep and made sure there was no pushing on line.

"Only one jump each," she told the sheep. "One jump and that's it!" (Of course, if a little lamb missed, she might give him another chance.)

But it wasn't working. Her usual way of counting sheep didn't make her feel sleepy at all. Not tonight.

So Angela counted sheep jumping on top of Tina. As she drifted off to sleep, there was a big pile of sheep with Tina squirming around someplace underneath. . . .

Pulling Together

As they talked in the kitchen, Tina and Nathaniel helped their mother with the dishes.

"I don't understand, Mom," Tina said. "How come you haven't been picked to serve on a jury yet?"

"Well," her mother said, "I did go to some panels. You see, the lawyers for both sides interview prospective jurors for a case, but I wasn't chosen."

"Were your feelings hurt?" Tina asked.

Her mother laughed. "Well, strangely enough, they were."

"I hope you get on a murder trial," Nathaniel said.

"I'm not sure I could take that," their mother said. "Well," she said, "someone told me that if I wasn't picked for a case by Friday, they'd probably tell me to go home. I'd be dismissed."

"Oh, Mom!" Tina felt disappointed. She hoped her mother would be chosen for something.

"Mom," Tina said, glancing at Nathaniel, "if we said 'seventeen dollars a month' to you, would you think that was a lot of money?"

Her mother was quiet for a moment.

"Well, it *is* a lot of money," her mother said, "but it depends what it's for."

"Let's say," Tina said slowly, "it was to save someone's life."

"No amount of money is too much to save a human life," her mother said. "Human lives can't be measured in money. . . ." She stopped and looked at Tina. "Sorry, Tina," she said. "I guess I got carried away. I have a feeling I'm not answering your question."

"That's okay," Tina said. "I was just wondering."

She looked over at Nathaniel, who had sat down at the table and was now reading an old copy of a science magazine called *Gee Whiz*. He didn't look up.

When Tina went to dump the garbage in the

hall, she noticed a sign next to the elevator:

HAVE ANY BABIES? HAVE ANY TODDLERS?
NEED A GOOD BABYSITTER?
Call 580-3254.

"That's *our* phone number!" Tina gasped. Then she realized Nathaniel must have put the sign up. Tina was amazed her brother worked so fast. She was very impressed.

She went back to the kitchen. Nathaniel was still sitting at the table reading his magazine.

"Mom!" Tina burst out. "Did you buy my Christmas present yet?"

"I couldn't. You have to come with me to try those boots on," her mother said.

"Could I have the fifty-five dollars instead?" Tina asked. "I'm saving up for something special."

"But you won't have a single present under the tree," her mother said. "That's the only present you wanted."

"I'm getting too old to care about presents," Tina said. "Oh, please!"

"Money doesn't seem very Christmassy," her mother said slowly. "But, if you're sure . . ."

"I'm sure," Tina said.

When her mother left the kitchen, Tina whispered to Nathaniel.

"I saw your sign. Thanks."

"I didn't do it for you," Nathaniel mumbled. "I want to rescue a child, too."

"I know," Tina said. "And with the money I get for Christmas, we'll save up and get an orphan next year. You were right. Next year is okay."

Nathaniel just grunted and kept reading.

Tina sat across from him at the table and started a new letter to Mrs. Glenn.

"How does this sound?" she asked.

And she read, " 'If it is possible, could you please reserve an orphan for our family for next year? We are positive we will be in a position to support a child at that time. . . .' "

"I'm not sure about the word 'positive,' " Nathaniel said.

Tina crossed out the word 'positive' and wrote in 'pretty sure.' Then she began copying the letter over—very neatly.

"I think you should see if Angela's still awake," Nathaniel said.

"Why?" Tina asked.

"I think you should tell her you're sorry you called her a spoiled little brat," Nathaniel told her.

"Look, Nathaniel," Tina said. "I have slightly more important things to think about. Right this very minute little children are suffering all over the world."

"Angela is suffering, too," Nathaniel said. "She was quiet all during dinner and she hardly ate anything."

Tina didn't answer.

"Oh, come on, Tina, you're six years older than Angela. Besides, you know what they say about people in the same family and how they should never go to bed mad at each other."

"And why not?" Tina asked coldly.

"I guess because one of them might wake up dead," Nathaniel said.

Tina snorted. "You don't believe that, do you? That's just an old superstition. Anyway, how do you 'wake up dead'?"

Nathaniel just shrugged. "Have it your own way, Tina," he said, and he went to bed.

"Wake up dead?" Tina snorted again. "That's ridiculous!"

Late that night Tina went into Angela's room.

86

Angela was asleep. Tina sat on the bed and put her hand on Angela's back to make sure she was breathing.

"Tina?" Angela mumbled. "I'm-sorry-about-the-sheep-and-I-hope-you-get-an-orphan."

Tina didn't understand about the sheep, but she said, "I'm the one who's sorry!" She knew Angela wasn't really awake so it didn't count.

Tina stayed there for a long time with her hand on Angela's back. She didn't want to take any chances.

The Last
Show and Tell

Tina took good care of Angela Wednesday morning. They were both very excited when they saw it was snowing.

Then Tina realized she would have to wear her brown rubber boots. She took them out of the green plastic bag with the clothes for the Christmas Drive. For a brief moment Tina regretted having given up her Christmas present. She might never get suede boots in her entire life. She might have to wear rubber boots over her shoes until the day she died.

Tina grabbed the green plastic bag. On the way out the door, she noticed a letter addressed to her in her mother's handwriting. There was no time to read it now, so Tina stuck it into her book bag.

It wasn't until they were already in the elevator that Tina remembered her letter to Mrs. Glenn.

"I forgot something," Tina said to Angela, "but I guess it doesn't really matter. I don't need it." Tina decided she would just tell Mrs. Glenn that her family simply did not have the money to rescue a child this Christmas.

"I forgot something, too," Angela said.

"What did you forget?" Tina asked.

"I forgot my Show and Tell," Angela said. "Today is Show and Tell, but I guess I'll have to wait until next Wednesday."

"There's no school next Wednesday," Tina told her. "It's the first day of Christmas vacation. This is the last Show and Tell before Christmas vacation."

The last Show and Tell? Angela swallowed hard, but she didn't want to be late for school.

When the elevator reached the lobby, Tina looked at her watch. It was ten to nine. They were very late. Melissa probably wouldn't speak to her for the rest of the day.

Tina looked down at Angela.

"We're going back," she suddenly said. She pushed the elevator button. "We're getting you something for Show and Tell."

"Oh, thank you, Tina!" Angela said.

Angela looked around her room for something very special for the last Show and Tell before Christmas.

Nothing seemed special enough. She found herself gazing at Stuffed Elephant and thought how nice he looked with his red bow and the red pads on his feet. What a treat he would be for Miss Berry's kindergarten! How thoughtful of Angela to want to share him with the class!

"Are you sure?" Tina asked when she saw what Angela had chosen. "Are you sure you want to take Stuffed Elephant to school?"

"Yes," Angela said.

Tina found another plastic bag for Angela so Stuffed Elephant would not get snow all over him. Besides, Angela did not want to put him in a bag full of old clothes.

Angela was terribly excited. She knew they had to hurry, but she tried to walk very smoothly so Stuffed Elephant wouldn't get bounced around.

As they turned the corner of their building,

Tina could see Sarah waiting for her in the snow.

Melissa wasn't even there.

"She's home pretending to be sick," Sarah explained. "Her mother's going to be at school today helping with this Christmas Drive. Melissa said she wouldn't be caught dead there. She's so embarrassed."

Sarah glanced shyly at Tina. "You must be very proud of *your* mother."

Tina's mouth fell open. "Why?" she asked.

"I saw it on the *Morning News*," Sarah said.

"On television?" Tina stared at Sarah.

Angela wasn't the least bit surprised to hear the *Morning News* had covered her mother going to jury duty. She was just sorry she had missed it.

Tina came to her senses. "*What* did you see on the *Morning News*?" she asked Sarah.

"Well, the Mayor said he was opening fifty new shelters for homeless people all over the city," Sarah told Tina. "He said he had gotten thousands of letters from concerned citizens."

Tina suddenly threw her arms around Sarah. "Oh, that's wonderful!" she shouted. "Wait until Mom hears about it."

"Shouldn't we hurry?" Angela asked.

Tina and Sarah looked at each other.

"We're already late, I think," Sarah said.

"Mr. Glaser's going to be furious," Tina added.

The three girls ran the rest of the way.

Angela walked into her kindergarten class and saw all the children gathered together in a circle. Even Eddie Bishop was sitting quietly. Sharing Circle had already begun!

But Miss Berry gave Angela a big smile, and said, "Well, isn't that nice. Look, class. Angela remembered!"

What did I remember? Angela wondered.

"We can't wait to see what you brought," Miss Berry said. "Can we, class?"

Well, of course I remembered Show and Tell! Angela thought, but, at the same time, she was pleased to see that a big fuss was being made over the last Show and Tell before Christmas. That was as it should be, she told herself.

She took off her raincoat and boots. She did not take Stuffed Elephant out of the plastic bag. She did not want to spoil the surprise. Then she tiptoed over to the circle and sat down next to Cheryl. Angela noticed that Cheryl was holding a paper bag on her lap.

Angela was curious. Cheryl usually brought wonderful things for Show and Tell. Last week it was a baby doll that could drink from a bottle and burp. The week before Cheryl had brought in a magician's kit and performed magic tricks for the class. But Angela knew that, no matter what Cheryl had brought today, it could not possibly be better than Stuffed Elephant.

"Now, Cheryl," Miss Berry said. "Stand up and tell the class what you brought."

Cheryl smoothed out her plaid skirt and stood up. She reached into her paper bag.

"I brought this can of peas," Cheryl said.

A can of peas for Show and Tell? Angela gasped. Then she realized it must be a trick can of peas. Angela folded her hands on her lap and waited politely for Cheryl to do her magic trick with the can of peas.

"Peas are full of vitamins and good things to eat and I hope a poor person will enjoy what I brought for the Drive," Cheryl said.

"Thank you, Cheryl." Miss Berry seemed delighted. "Thank you for remembering those who have less to eat. Now put your gift on our display table for the Christmas Drive."

For the first time, Angela noticed that the art

table by the window was covered with clothes, cans of food, and old toys.

"You said you weren't going to bring anything," Angela whispered angrily to Cheryl when Cheryl had sat down again. "I thought you hated poor people."

Cheryl giggled. "I hate peas too," she whispered back. "I hope Eddie's family gets them and Eddie has to eat them."

Angela watched in horror as other children showed what they had brought for the Christmas Drive for the Needy. Meredith had brought a small blue sweater "to keep a poor child warm," she said primly.

Even Eddie had brought something. When his turn came, he ran to his cubby and pulled out a man's woolen scarf. It was so worn you could see through it in some places.

"This is for some poor kid's father," he said hoarsely, "so he won't get cold while he's looking for a job." He took the scarf and laid it down very gently on the art table.

For a moment Angela thought Miss Berry had tears in her eyes. "Thank you, Eddie," was all she said.

Angela felt as if a net were tightening around

her. She wanted to run. . . .

"Angela," Miss Berry said. "Show us what you have brought now."

Angela got to her feet. She felt like a robot. She pulled Stuffed Elephant out of the plastic bag. Then she just stood there holding him out in front of her.

Miss Berry smiled encouragingly. "Yes, Angela?"

"This is an elephant," Angela whispered, "but . . ." Her throat went dry. She stared at the floor.

"Is that all you want to say?" Miss Berry asked.

Angela nodded. Her cheeks were burning.

"It's a lovely elephant." Miss Berry smiled. "I'm sure it will make some child very happy on Christmas morning. Thank you for remembering those children who are less fortunate than ourselves."

Angela walked stiffly to the art table. She put Stuffed Elephant down next to a raggedy teddy bear with dirty matted fur and no eyes.

Then she walked stiffly back to her place in the circle without looking back.

Late!

Tina and Sarah arrived at the door to their classroom ten minutes late.

Mr. Glaser looked up from his desk and saw them standing outside the classroom. He came out into the hall.

"Well, ladies?" Mr. Glaser looked very displeased.

"It was my fault," Tina said quickly. "I was late and Sarah had to wait for me."

"Go inside and take your seat, Sarah," Mr. Glaser said sternly. "And, in the future, please remember that loyalty to a friend is no excuse for being late."

After Sarah had gone inside, Mr. Glaser said,

"Now, Tina, perhaps you'll tell me why *you* were late."

"I don't really have an excuse," Tina admitted. "I guess I just wasted a lot of time. You see, my mother had to leave early for jury duty and then my little sister forgot her Show and Tell. . . ."

"Your mother's on jury duty?" Mr. Glaser asked.

Tina nodded proudly. "I hope she gets on a case, though. I hope they don't let her off."

"No kidding?" Mr. Glaser smiled. Tina thought her teacher had a very nice smile. "Why didn't you say something before, Tina?" he asked her.

Tina just said, "I don't know."

"I was on jury duty this summer," Mr. Glaser told her, "on a murder trial. We were even sequestered overnight."

Tina was curious. "What does *sequestered* mean?" she asked Mr. Glaser.

Mr. Glaser thought for a moment. "I guess it means keeping the members of a jury away from the rest of the world. When the time came for us to make our decision, we were not allowed to talk to anyone except other members of the jury. They don't want anyone trying to influence your decision — not even your family and friends."

"How do they do that?" Tina asked him.

"Well, they locked us in the jury room to talk it over. All twelve members have to agree in a criminal case, but at the end of the day our jury still couldn't agree. . . ." Mr. Glaser paused and looked into the classroom. "Dinnertime came. . . ."

Tina saw that her whole class had stopped working. They were staring at Tina and Mr. Glaser through the door window.

"Go ahead." Tina wanted to hear the rest of the story. "Then dinnertime came . . ."

". . . and we were taken to a restaurant," Mr. Glaser went on. "We had to eat dinner surrounded by guards. We weren't even allowed to call home; the guards had to call our families for us. That night we slept in a hotel locked in our rooms. The phones were cut off. The TV sets had been removed. We had no communication with the outside world!"

Tina shivered. It was one of the most exciting stories she had ever heard. Mr. Glaser seemed to be enjoying telling her about it.

"The next morning," he went on, "we were taken back to the courthouse and locked up in the jury room again. We didn't reach a decision until four o'clock that afternoon."

Suddenly Mr. Glaser seemed very embarrassed. His face was bright red. "I didn't mean to talk your ear off, Tina," he said. He looked at his watch. Then he grinned at Tina. "I'm sorry I held you up," he said.

He held the door to the classroom open and Tina walked in carrying the green garbage bag.

Tina knew the whole class was watching her take off her coat and boots. She felt her face getting redder and redder. She took her notebook out of her book bag and sat down at her desk. The girl behind her started poking her.

"Tina, Tina, Tina," Linda whispered loudly. "What was he saying to you? Why was he blushing? What's going on between you two?"

Tina tried to ignore her. Linda was the biggest nosybody in the whole school.

Tina opened her book bag. The letter from her mother dropped out of it and fell on the floor. Tina picked it up and tried to hide it in her notebook, but Linda had already seen it.

"Who wrote you that letter?" Linda demanded to know. "Aren't you going to open it? It's a love letter, right?"

"It's from my mother," Tina whispered over her shoulder.

"Sure, Tina, sure," Linda muttered. "Your own mother wrote you a letter. Do you expect me to believe that?"

Tina tried to concentrate on what Mr. Glaser was saying, but Linda was making it very difficult.

"He just smiled at you again." Now Linda was tapping her on the shoulder. "Oh, come on, Tina," she whined, "just tell me what he was saying to you in the hall. I promise I won't tell anyone!"

Tina gave up. "We were just talking about being *sequestered*," she whispered.

Linda nearly fainted. By the time the class had split up into math groups, Linda had told everyone that Tina and Mr. Glaser had become *sequestered*. . . .

"It's something like being engaged to be engaged," Tina heard Linda explain to someone in her math group. "Maybe it's more like going steady . . . but now that I think of it, I'm pretty sure my sister told me that you got sequestered first—then you go steady. . . ."

Tina was beginning to find the whole thing pretty funny.

The Rewards

During free play, Angela sat at a table very close to Miss Berry's desk and waited. She was waiting for Miss Berry to come over to her. She was waiting for Miss Berry to say, "I can't let you give up your stuffed elephant, Angela. It's much too much to give. Please take it back."

Miss Berry was very busy at her desk, but she looked up a few times to ask Angela if she were feeling all right. Angela was afraid to look over at Stuffed Elephant. She was afraid she was letting him down. She decided to take a little peek just to see how much nicer he was than anything else on the table.

She turned around and saw Eddie standing in

front of the table. He was petting Stuffed Elephant. He was getting his germs all over Stuffed Elephant.

Angela ran to the art table.

"Don't touch him," she said.

Eddie pulled his hand away and held it behind his back. He stared at Angela.

"He's for a poor kid, right?" Eddie asked in his hoarse voice.

"For someone less fortunate," Angela told him, and she wondered if Eddie knew he was poor. *He might even be less fortunate*, she thought. The idea surprised her.

"You're crazy to give that elephant away," Eddie told her.

Angela nodded. She agreed with him.

"I guess I'm crazy, too," Eddie said.

He was no longer looking at Stuffed Elephant. He was looking at the scarf he had given to the Christmas Drive.

Suddenly Angela had a funny feeling about that scarf. She looked at Eddie.

Eddie shrugged his shoulders. "My grandmother says he can get a new one if he comes back."

"Who?" Angela asked him.

"My dad," Eddie said. "He doesn't live with us anymore."

Angela was quiet.

"Oh, well." Eddie sighed. "You're supposed to give the best thing you have, anyway."

"You are?" Angela asked.

"Of course," Eddie said. "If you give the best thing you have, it does more good."

Angela looked straight at Stuffed Elephant—right into his wise blue eyes.

She fixed his red bow and went to find something to do.

Angela was sitting at a table patting a piece of clay when Cheryl leaned over and whispered loudly, "I hate to tell you, Angela, but Eddie Bishop is sitting next to you."

Angela did not even look up from her lump of clay.

While they were lining up for lunch, Cheryl turned to Angela and said, "You know, Angela, I'm not even sure I want that strawberry sticker. I'm thinking about changing my mind."

Angela was amazed. Maybe there *were* rewards in life. After all, she had given the best thing she had to the Christmas Drive.

"Miss Berry!" Cheryl called sweetly. "I'm letting Angela have the strawberry sticker."

Eddie made a funny sound. "Well, I guess there goes my car sticker," he whispered. Angela looked at him. He shrugged and looked out the window. He seemed to be daydreaming. He had never really expected to get his own smelly sticker.

Cheryl tapped Angela on the shoulder. "You can have it, Angela. I don't even want the strawberry anymore."

Angela whirled around. "Too bad for you," she told Cheryl. "I don't want it either."

Cheryl was so surprised she just stood there with her mouth hanging open. Miss Berry looked as if she were trying hard not to laugh.

Tina's sixth grade class was getting ready to go to lunch, too.

"Tina," Sarah said. "I just want you to know I don't believe a word Linda is saying about that letter from Mr. Glaser. *I* know it's not a love letter."

Tina opened the letter her mother had left for her that morning.

"What does it say, anyway?" Sarah asked.

Tina read it to herself:

Dear Tina —

Mrs. Glenn called last night after you were in bed. She wanted to tell me what lovely children I had. Then she said that she hadn't meant to talk so much about the Rescue the Children Program. Melissa had been quite angry at her when they got home.

"Tina," Sarah said. "I just want you to know that you don't have to tell me what's in the letter."

"Huh?" Tina asked. She stared at Sarah with a dazed expression and went back to reading the letter.

It didn't take long to figure out what was going on. After all, you had given up your Christmas present. I knew you and Nathaniel were trying to raise money for something.

In any case, I told Mrs. Glenn I knew all about it, and that we would be delighted to sponsor a child. I am sure you and Nathaniel will be able to earn part of the cost of sponsoring a child each month. We will pay the rest. We want to help, too. I know both of you will be

doing the best you can, and that is
what matters.

Here is a check for the first month.
That will give us time to get organized.
I told Mrs. Glenn you would give it to
her at lunchtime.

Your loving Mom

P.S. Mrs. Glenn tells me you have
very sophisticated taste. Did you
really eat eels?

Tina peeked in the envelope and saw a pink
check. She read the letter again. She clasped the
letter to her heart. Then she noticed Sarah staring at her.

"Tina!" Sarah said sharply. "Your eyes are all
sparkly. Is it a love letter?"

"Yes," Tina sighed again. "Well, in a way. . . ."

Angela sat in the Little Cafeteria eating her
lunch. Only the lower grades ate there.

Eddie sat down next to her. "If you get me
that car sticker, you can sniff it all the time if you
want to," he told Angela.

Angela shook her head. "No one should ever
sniff it more than once a day," she told Eddie.
"You don't want to wear it out."

"Angela!" Tina was calling her. Angela was surprised. Tina never came into the Little Cafeteria.

"Come with me!" Tina called. "You have to help me fill out the forms. We're getting an orphan *right this minute.*"

Angela went with Tina to a table outside the cafeteria. She felt confused. She saw Melissa's mother standing at the table wearing a bright green suit and a Christmas corsage.

"I hear you're going to be a proud parent, too!" Mrs. Glenn smiled at Angela.

"Me?" Angela said. Suddenly she understood. They were going to rescue a child. And Tina was sharing the orphan with her!

Tina's hand was shaking as she filled out the form. "Do we want a boy or a girl?" she asked Angela.

"A girl would be nice," Angela said. "No, maybe a boy. . . ."

"Should I check 'Either One'?"

"Yes," Angela said shyly.

"What country?" Tina asked her. She read off the list of countries, but Angela hadn't heard of any of them.

"Maybe I should check 'Wherever There Is the

Most Need,' " Tina said. "What do you think?"

"Yes," Angela said. "Check that."

"I think Nathaniel would want us to do that," Tina said. Then she wrote in the name of everyone in their family. She handed Mrs. Glenn the form and the pink check.

"Congratulations!" Mrs. Glenn said.

Tina and Angela hugged each other. Then Tina went to tell Sarah the whole story.

Angela just stood at the table looking shyly up at Melissa's mother.

"Do you know Theresa?" she asked Mrs. Glenn.

"Who?" Mrs. Glenn asked her.

"Theresa," Angela said. "Do you know her?"

"Oh, you mean our poster child?"

Angela nodded.

"I understand she was adopted by a family a few months ago," Mrs. Glenn told Angela.

"Does she have shoes now?" Angela asked.

"Yes," Mrs. Glenn said. "I'm sure she does. I think Theresa will be having a very nice Christmas this year."

"Well, say hello to her for me," Angela said, and she ran to catch up with Tina.

O Stuffed Elephant

At the end of the day, Miss Berry packed all the things for the Christmas Drive into boxes. It was a very sad sight, but Angela watched. She had to make sure Miss Berry did not squish Stuffed Elephant's trunk. Then she turned away and went to meet Tina.

Tina was waiting for her at the end of the hall. As soon as Angela saw her, she started to run.

"Tina!" she shouted. "Guess what. Eddie got a check mark today. If he gets one every day for the rest of the week, he'll get his own smelly sticker. He got a check mark!"

"He did?" Tina smiled.

"Yes, he really did." Angela was very excited.

"He was so busy watching me be good, he forgot to be bad! And here's the best part: Everyone in the whole kindergarten is hoping he'll get his own smelly sticker. Miss Berry hopes so. I hope so. Even Cheryl hopes so!"

"What about Eddie?" Tina asked.

"Oh, he's just happy everyone is hoping *for* him," Angela told her. "He said today felt like Christmas."

When Tina and Angela got home from school their mother was in the living room talking to Nathaniel. Tina felt a little disappointed. Her mother wasn't on jury duty after all.

"But I am!" her mother said. "I was picked for a jury this morning. The trial doesn't start until the Monday after New Year's because of the Christmas recess."

"Oh, Mom!" Tina was delighted. "We'll help with the housework. We'll help with everything!"

"I'll do all the shopping," Angela promised.

"No, you won't!" everyone said at once.

"Nathaniel got a job," their mother said proudly. "A babysitting job—two afternoons a week."

"That's wonderful!" Tina said. "Who hired you, Nathaniel?"

"I'll tell you in a minute," Nathaniel said. "I

have to find out something first." He turned to his mother. "Oh, come on, Mom," he pleaded. "Please tell me what the case is about. I've already guessed murder, robbery, burglary, attempted murder. . . ."

"She's not supposed to talk about it," Tina told Nathaniel.

"I know," Nathaniel muttered. "That's what she keeps telling me."

"If I say one word to you, Nathaniel," his mother said, "you'll have everything out of me in no time."

Nathaniel was gazing at his mother. "I'll bet it's armed robbery. It *is* armed robbery, isn't it, Mom?"

"Oh honestly, Nathaniel," his mother said. She looked very flushed and excited.

They had pizza for dinner that night. The pizza was covered with red and green peppers.

"Christmas pizza," Angela said happily.

The phone kept ringing during dinner. Melissa called a few times to find out the real story about Tina and Mr. Glaser.

"Don't forget, Tina," Melissa said. "Teachers don't make that much money."

Then Sarah called to tell Tina that she had fixed up her room in case the orphan came to visit.

Right in the middle of dinner, their father arrived home from his trip.

Angela ran down the hall to meet him.

"Daddy!" she shouted. "Guess what! We're adopting a child, but we don't know who it is yet! And guess what else! Mommy's not going to jail!"

Angela enjoyed surprising people. She was pleased to see that her father was looking very surprised indeed. He dropped his suitcase and cello case, picked up Angela, and held her in his arms. He held her tight. All at once Angela realized how glad she was to see him, how much she had missed him.

"I forgot to say welcome home," she said.

"I'm glad to *be* home," her father whispered in her ear.

After dinner Tina and Nathaniel sat in the living room listening to the music from *The Nut-cracker Suite* on the record player.

"How did Daddy know we wanted that record?" Tina couldn't get over it. "He didn't even know we had seen the ballet!"

Their parents were in the kitchen talking. Angela was in bed.

Tina suddenly felt happy, excited, and scared— all at the same time.

"Nathaniel," she said slowly. "Do you think that maybe this Christmas Spirit that everyone talks about is just *hoping*?"

"What do you mean?" Nathaniel asked.

"Just hoping . . . hoping to rescue a child; hoping everyone in the world will have enough to eat. And Angela's kindergarten class— all hoping Eddie will get his smelly sticker."

"Maybe," Nathaniel said.

"Not *getting* all those things," Tina went on. "Not even *wishing* for them. Just hoping. Everybody hoping. . . ."

Angela lay in her bed holding her white lamb whose name was Gambi.

Gambi was not taking Stuffed Elephant's place. No animal would ever take Stuffed Elephant's place. But Angela had chosen to sleep with Gambi tonight because she knew Gambi missed Stuffed Elephant, too.

Angela closed her eyes tight.

"O Stuffed Elephant," she prayed, "wherever you may be . . . I miss you very much. Gambi misses you, too. I hope you are all right. I hope your new child will be very surprised to see you on Christmas morning, and I hope . . ."

Tina passed Angela's door on her way to bed.

"Well, Stuffed Elephant," she heard Angela saying, "I guess I talked to you long enough."

Tina smiled and tiptoed away.

". . . and I'll tell you the rest tomorrow," Angela went on sleepily, "wherever you may be."

About the Author

NANCY K. ROBINSON writes with a special blend of humor and insight into what really matters to young children. "Children are my favorite audience," she says. "I like to write about problems that confused me when I was a child and still confuse me now."

This particular book was inspired by something that happened to Ms. Robinson's younger sister. As a child, her sister actually had a stuffed elephant like the one that figures prominently in this book. How she felt about that stuffed elephant, and what happened to it, are mirrored in the things that happen in this story.

Ms. Robinson's other books include *Just Plain Cat, Veronica the Show-off,* and *Wendy and the Bullies.*